The Adventures of
Underwater Dog

The Adventures

For Mary Jack Wald
—J. W.

To Jessica, Jasmine, and Frankie
—T. B.

Text copyright © 1989 by Jan Wahl.
Illustrations copyright © 1989 by Tim Bowers.
All rights reserved. Published by Grosset & Dunlap, Inc.,
a member of The Putnam Publishing Group, New York.
Published simultaneously in Canada. Printed and bound in Singapore.
Library of Congress Catalog Card Number: 88-81173
ISBN 0-448-09313-8   A B C D E F G H I J

Underwater Dog

By Jan Wahl
Illustrated by Tim Bowers

Publishers · GROSSET & DUNLAP · New York
A member of The Putnam Publishing Group

Some people say his real name was Fred and that even as a pup he liked to splash in the tub.

They say he grew up in a red lighthouse
and one day he just rowed away to live on his
own, as best he could.

He looked for sand dollars until he saved enough to buy flippers, goggles, and a rubber snorkel.

And then he became the one we all know
and love. None other than ...
Underwater Dog!

One day, on the pier, the bakery was robbed
by thugs wearing bowler hats and ski masks.
They ran fast with the cash box. Also
fourteen dozen doughnuts.

A trail of delicious crumbs led off the dock.
"This is a job for Underwater Dog!" said
Underwater Dog.
And he snorkeled away out of sight.

The thugs were in a submarine, dunking doughnuts and counting money from the cash box.

Underwater Dog, swimming at top speed,
saw the submarine. It looked *suspicious*.
He peeked in one porthole.
"Just as I thought!" chuckled Underwater Dog.

Cleverly, he unscrewed the propeller. And he
tied on a rope and pulled....

"It's Underwater Dog! We're sunk!" cried the nervous thugs.
They tried to swim away.

Luckily, Underwater Dog had a net. He threw it over them. Panting, he towed the thugs to shore.

The Chief of Police stood on the pier.
"I take off my hat to you, Underwater Dog!"

The reward was all the doughnuts he could eat.

THE LOST DIAMOND ADVENTURE

One day, a rich lady went diving off the deck
of her yacht.
   She wore a terrific, sparkling diamond.
   Whoops! The ring slipped off her
elegant paw.

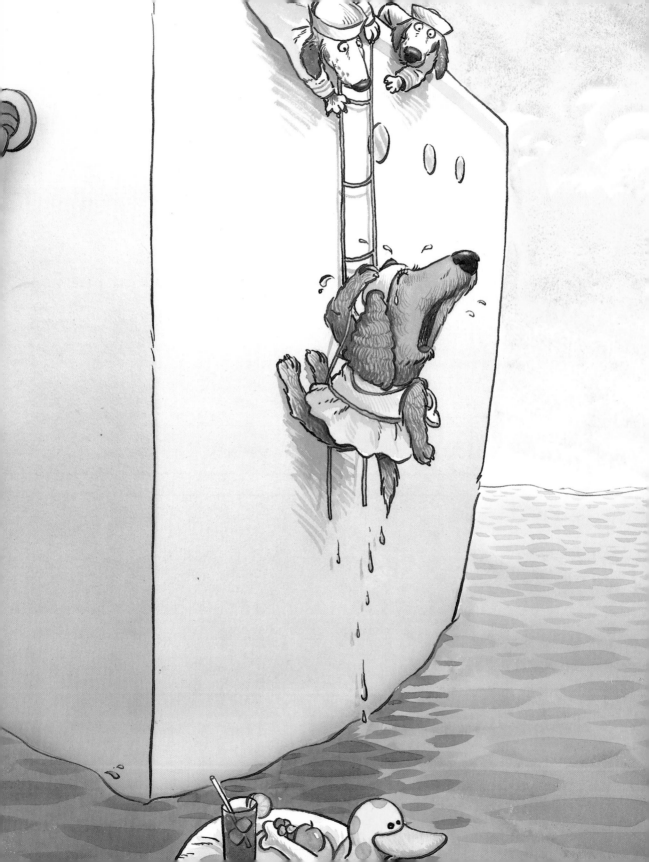

She shouted loudly as the sailors pulled her up, "HELP! Reward!"

Underwater Dog, swimming nearby, heard the cry for help.

"Do not fear, dear lady," he replied and down, down he dropped to the floor of the sea.

Five mermaids lay taking naps quietly.
He shook them and asked, "Did you find
a diamond ring?"

"*Diamond ring?*" they gasped.

They guessed they were dreaming and
went back to sleep.

On rushed Underwater Dog—flipping his flippers, looking under each shell and stone. The sun went down. A last ray of light hit the water. Underwater Dog paddled round and round.

A star was shining …
But not up in the dusky sky!
At the very bottom of the sea he found
the diamond.

Sailors pulled him aboard the yacht.
"Here's your reward, Underwater Dog," said
the rich lady. She gave him a hug.

And the mermaids got invited to the wedding.